The Best Place to Read

The Best Place to Read

by **Debbie Bertram** & **Susan Bloom** illustrated by **Michael Garland**

Dragonfly Books New York

All rights reserved. Published in the United States by Dragonfly Books, an imprint of
Random House Children's Books, a division of Random House, Inc., New York.
Originally published in hardcover in the United States by Random House Children's Books,
a division of Random House, Inc., New York, in 2003.

Dragonfly Books with the colophon is a registered trademark of Random House, Inc.

Visit us on the Web! www.randomhouse.com/kids

Educators and librarians, for a variety of teaching tools, visit us at
www.randomhouse.com/teachers

Library of Congress Cataloging-in-Publication Data
Bertram, Debbie.
The best place to read / by Debbie Bertram and Susan Bloom; illustrated by Michael Garland.
p. cm.
Summary: A young child with a new book hunts inside and outside the house
before finding the right chair for reading.
ISBN 978-0-375-82293-3 (trade) — ISBN 978-0-375-92293-0 (lib. bdg.) — ISBN 978-0-375-83757-9 (pbk.)
[1. Reading—Fiction. 2. Chairs—Fiction. 3. Mother and child—Fiction. 4. Stories in rhyme.]
I. Bloom, Susan. II. Garland, Michael, ill. III. Title.
PZ8.3.B4595 Bg 2003
[E]—dc21
2001050099

MANUFACTURED IN CHINA

14 13 12 11 10 9 8 7 6

To Arnie and Jordan,
Our husbands,
our cheerleaders,
our best friends
—With love,
Debbie and Susan

To my aunt Helen
—M.G.

A new book for me—
I can't wait to read!
I run to my own little chair.
I'm growing too tall and the seat is too small,
So I am not comfortable there.

Into the den—
That's a good place to read.
I love Grammy's soft, cozy chair.
But so does old Rover. I tell him, "Move over,"
But he won't make room for me there.

Three eggs.

Daddy's chair must be magic—
The seat can move back, up, and down
In this big leather chair.
A cool, windy feeling—the fan on the ceiling
Is spinning and blasting cold air.

Snack time! I'm hungry—
I'll read in the kitchen.
Baby's booster is next to my chair.
The table's so sticky, my hands get all icky—
YUCK! Why would I want to read there?

Grandpa looks comfy
Whenever he reads
In his lumpy and bumpy old chair.
My book drops to my feet when springs poke through
    the seat—BOING!
I bounce up so high in the air.

Upstairs! I'll read
In my big brother's room.
I flop on his round beanbag chair.
Surprise! I yell, "EEK!" as the chair springs
    a leak—
There are beans and more beans everywhere.

Her Highness, the Princess—
That's my big sis.
A gold seat like a throne is her chair.
But her stereo's singing, her telephone's ringing—
Too loud! Who could ever read there?

So back down the stairs—
Oh, where can I read?
In Auntie's old wood rocking chair.
Like a rocking machine, I feel seasick and green.
I have to go out for some air.

The backyard is great—
I can read on the grass.
I'll sit on a patio chair.
It's the sprinklers—OH, NO!—splashing me head to toe,
So now it's too wet to read there.

I dry myself off.
I give up, I can't read.
I've tried to sit down everywhere.
With no reading done, I'm still on page one—
I *can't* find a comfortable chair!

"Mommy, oh, Mom!
May I sit on your lap?
I love it so much when we share."
The best place to be, just my book, Mom, and me—
At last . . .
In a comfortable chair.